Red
Wagon

Renata Liwska

PHILOMEL BOOKS
An Imprint of Penguin Group (USA) Inc.

To my mom, who set the red wagon in motion,
and to Courtenay, who helped to pull the wagon up the hill.

PHILOMEL BOOKS

A division of Penguin Young Readers Group.
Published by The Penguin Group.
Penguin Group (USA) Inc., 375 Hudson Street, New York, NY 10014, U.S.A.
Penguin Group (Canada), 90 Eglinton Avenue East, Suite 700, Toronto, Ontario M4P 2Y3, Canada (a division of Pearson Penguin Canada Inc.).
Penguin Books Ltd, 80 Strand, London WC2R 0RL, England.
Penguin Ireland, 25 St. Stephen's Green, Dublin 2, Ireland (a division of Penguin Books Ltd).
Penguin Group (Australia), 250 Camberwell Road, Camberwell, Victoria 3124, Australia (a division of Pearson Australia Group Pty Ltd).
Penguin Books India Pvt Ltd, 11 Community Centre, Panchsheel Park, New Delhi - 110 017, India.
Penguin Group (NZ), 67 Apollo Drive, Rosedale, North Shore 0632, New Zealand (a division of Pearson New Zealand Ltd).
Penguin Books (South Africa) (Pty) Ltd, 24 Sturdee Avenue, Rosebank, Johannesburg 2196, South Africa.
Penguin Books Ltd, Registered Offices: 80 Strand, London WC2R 0RL, England.

Published simultaneously in Canada. Manufactured in China by South China Printing Co. Ltd.

Design by Ryan Thomann. Text set in Metallophile.
The illustrations were rendered with pencil and colored digitally.

Library of Congress Cataloging-in-Publication Data
Liwska, Renata. Red wagon / Renata Liwska.—1st ed. p. cm.
Summary: When Lucy gets a new red wagon she wants to play with it immediately,
but first she must use it to bring vegetables home from the market for her mother.
[1. Wagons—Fiction. 2. Work—Fiction. 3. Play—Fiction.] I. Title.
PZ7.L7652Re 2011 [E]—dc22 2010005393
ISBN 978-0-399-25575-5
1 3 5 7 9 10 8 6 4 2

Lucy had a brand-new little red wagon.

She wanted to play with it immediately.
She asked her mother.

"Sure, you can use your wagon to go to the market."

That sounded like a chore.
Lucy didn't want to do chores.

But she set out to the market.
She pulled her red wagon up the hill.

It was pretty heavy.

At the top of the hill,
it started to rain!

Oh, bother.

Lucy quickly pushed
the wagon down the hill.

By the time she got to the bottom,
it was really coming down!

Soon the rain stopped and the sun came out.

She continued on her way.

At last, Lucy arrived at the market!

Lucy neatly loaded the wagon
with the vegetables from her list.

And she hauled them back up the hill.

She was almost down again
when the wagon hit a rock!

Luckily, the wagon was okay.

So was Lucy.

She gathered the vegetables
and put them back into her wagon.

When she got home,
her mother was waiting for her.

"Thank you, Lucy. What a big help!"

Finally, Lucy was free to play
with her wagon.